Praise for the Series

"*These are the stories I've been waiting to read since childhood — classic tales, vividly retold, and beautifully illustrated in ways that stimulate the imagination. The questions posed are important ones to young minds — how things happen and why, as well as the consequences of personal choices. They are what I pondered as a child experiencing my own twists and turns in life. And those were the thoughts that very much influenced my becoming a writer. As these stories show, there are no simple answers, but with imagination you can go to many places and find many possibilities. These are magical stories for everyone.*"

— Amy Tan
Award winning and best-selling writer
Author of "The Joy Luck Club"
Creative Consultant to the PBS television series "Sagwa"

"*As* a child, these tales nourished my imagination and ability to love and to hate. They introduced me to fantasy lands full of characters with courage, integrity and goodness. They made me understand that tragedies are not necessarily sad, because tender hearts usually achieve happiness and satisfaction through sorrow. In a word, they have made me what I am today, a writer, whose livelihood depends on compassion and fascination.

As modern renditions and artful adaptations of these ancient tales, this series has brought out the most touching elements and core spirit, drama and beauty of the old stories, yet at the same time given them a new life and charm catered to young readers today."

— **Geling Yan**
Award winning writer
Author of "The Banquet Bug"

"*As* my daughters are getting older, I have been wanting them to know the best stories from the Chinese culture, but have found it hard to locate a version with the right kind of story-telling suitable to their ages and 'American' taste, that could draw and hold their attention, and strike a chord in their hearts.

I am happy to have been presented this series. Beautiful stories beautifully retold, in a refreshing way and with age appropriate gradings, this edition is the finest I've ever seen, definitely something I would like my children to read and grow up on."

— **Joan Chen**
Award winning actress/director
Leading role, "The Last Emperor"

The Girl Who Flew to the Moon

嫦娥奔月

Teri Tao

 Golden Peach Publishing

EUCLID

Text and illustrations copyright © 2008 by Golden Peach Publishing LLC

Published by Golden Peach Publishing LLC
1223 Wilshire Blvd., #1510
Santa Monica, CA 90403, USA
www.goldenpeachbooks.com
editorial@goldenpeachbooks.com

ISBN: 978-1-930655-03-4
Printed in China
First printing, May 2008

Editing, translation and notes by Nina Tao
English copy-editing by Rashid Williams-Garcia
Illustrations by Mango Li
Book design by Yang Hui

Long ago in ancient China, the top warrior in charge of guarding the Emperor of Heaven was Hou-Yi; the prettiest celestial girl was Chang'E.

As the best arrow shooter in the immortal world, Hou-Yi was so tough and strong that he was never afraid of anything...until the day he met Chang'E at a ball of the gods. In spite of himself, his face would turn red and his heart would pound heavily at the sight and thought of Chang'E. He went out of his way to pick a thousand-year-old peony for her in the Queen Mother of Heaven's secret garden, but she would not even give it one look. He tried with all his might to break several records at an arrow shooting meet, but she ignored him all the same. How could he ever make this girl pay any attention to him?

远古的时候，天帝身边的众多天神里，最强壮的勇士叫后羿，最漂亮的仙女叫嫦娥。后羿是天庭的神箭手。他性格豪爽，力大无比，什么都不怕。可自从在天庭舞会上认识嫦娥之后，每次看到、甚至想到嫦娥，他都会脸红心跳。他闯进王母娘娘的后花园，摘来千年牡丹，嫦娥看也没看；他在天庭射箭比赛中连破记录，抱回一把金牌，嫦娥理也不理。女孩子的心，真是摸不透啊！

In those days there were ten suns working in the sky. As sons of the Emperor of Heaven, they took turns getting up everyday to light and warm up the world.

After a while, the suns started feeling too good about themselves for the power they had over things on Earth. In spite of their father's repeated orders, they began coming up together, fighting with one another over which one of them was the most powerful.

With ten suns up in the sky at the same time, their flames burned up mountains and dried up waters in a matter of minutes. The Earth soon became a barren, deserted place. All the gods were worried.

那时候，天上有十个太阳。他们是天帝的儿子，在天帝的指挥下轮流出来，照亮人间，温暖大地。后来，十个太阳看到万物都要依靠它们生长，开始骄傲起来。他们不听天帝的指挥，开始成群结队，每天一起来到天上，争着显示自己的威力。他们喷出的火焰烤焦了山，烤干了水，大地一片荒凉。天神们都为此忧心忡忡。

The Emperor of Heaven was enraged with his sons' behavior. He gathered all the gods together and asked, "These urchins would not listen to me. Which of you could go down to Earth to help me get rid of them and save the world from suffering?"

The gods were all afraid to do anything to the Emperor's sons so they all kept quiet for a while.

"I'll go!" Hou-Yi stood out from the crowd and exclaimed.

One of the gods whispered to the Emperor of Heaven, "Hou Yi is brave and loyal, but he is too rash to take on a mission like this alone."

天帝也气急了。他把天神们召集到一处，问："这些捣蛋鬼根本不听我的。谁能下凡去除掉他们，解除人间的苦难？"天神们都顾及太阳是天帝的儿子，没人回答。"我去！"随着一声高喊，后羿站了出来。一位天神低声对天帝说："后羿勇猛忠诚，只是做事鲁莽，他一个人下凡恐怕不妥。"

"I'll go too." There came a soft but firm girl's voice.

Everybody turned to see Chang'E walking out from behind the clouds, her long sash fluttering in the wind. Hou-Yi was stunned.

Chang'E said to the Emperor, "I cannot bear to see the creatures on Earth suffering like this. I'm willing to go down there to help Hou-Yi."

"But it will be too dangerous! You can't go!" Hou-Yi shouted. It had been his dream to be with Chang'E, but he just could not let this fragile-looking beauty be part of this risky job.

"I am not afraid," said Chang'E.

"我去。"一个轻柔但是坚定的声音传了过来。大家回头一看，嫦娥裙带飘飘，从云朵中走了出来。后羿愣住了。只听嫦娥对天帝说："我不忍心看到人间众生受苦，愿意下凡帮助后羿。""太危险了！你不能去！"后羿大喊起来。他做梦都想和嫦娥在一起，但是他决不能让这个瘦弱的女孩子跟着自己去赴汤蹈火。"我不怕。"嫦娥说。

So the Emperor of Heaven sent Hou-Yi and Chang'E down to Earth to deal with his guilty sons.

With his big red bow and huge white arrow bag on his shoulders, and the beautiful Chang'E by his side, Hou-Yi came down to the human world. All they saw were forests on fire, animals dying of hunger and heat, and humans struggling helplessly in despair.

Hou-Yi and Chang'E got down to work right away. They climbed tall mountains and crossed wide rivers to chase the suns, until they reached the edge of the East Sea.

于是，天帝就派后羿和嫦娥下凡来整治太阳。后羿挎着红色的神弓，背着白色的利箭，和美丽的嫦娥一起来到人间。他们看到成片的山林大火，草木都在燃烧，动物成批地死去，人类也在火海中痛苦地挣扎。后羿和嫦娥片刻都没停留，开始翻山越岭，日夜不停地追逐太阳，一直追到东海海边。

High up atop the palisades, the suns' flames burned scorching hot right above their heads. Hou-Yi angrily pulled out his bow and arrows, but Chang'E firmly held his hands down.

Chang'E turned around to talk to the suns: "Could you guys please come out one at a time? One sun would be enough to light and warm the world. Ten suns together are just too hot for the creatures of Earth!"

Completely ignoring her pleadings, the ten suns laughed boisterously and spurted their flames even higher.

他们站在高高的峭壁上，太阳的火焰就在他们头顶燃烧。后羿愤怒地拔出了弓箭，嫦娥按住了他的手。嫦娥转过身来，对太阳喊道："请你们一个个轮流出来好吗？一个太阳就可以给人间带来光亮和温暖，十个太阳太热了，人间生灵都受不了啊！"太阳们根本不听嫦娥的哀求和劝告，狂笑着把火焰喷得更高。

With that, the flames of Hou-Yi's anger also spurted up. He pulled open his ten-thousand pound bow and took out his one-thousand pound arrows, and aimed at the wildest sun of all.

Chang'E whispered by his side, "Don't kill them. Just drive them away."

Whoosh! Whoosh! Whoosh! Three magical arrows whizzed up to the sky. Three suns wailed and scurried away, holding on to their wounds. The seven suns that were left were still too hot to bear. Hou-Yi aimed and shot six more arrows, and six more suns rolled into the East Sea.

后羿更加愤怒了。他拉开红色的万斤神弓，取出白色的千斤利箭，瞄准了其中最骄横的一个太阳。嫦娥在身边连忙说："不要真的射死他们，把他们赶走就是了。""嗖！""嗖！""嗖！"后羿一连射出三箭，三个太阳大叫起来，捂住伤口逃跑了。七个太阳还是很热，后羿又连发六箭，六个太阳翻滚着掉到东海里。

When Hou-Yi raised his bow and arrow to aim at the last sun, he paused for a moment, and then put his weapons down. Chang'E flashed him a big smile.

The last sun, in panic, tried to follow the others to jump down into the sea, when Chang'E stopped him: "Please stay! We need you! Please just rise and fall by the Emperor's schedule. Then everything on Earth will be grateful to you again!"

Blushed, the last sun said, "I will behave from now on!"

后羿瞄准最后一个太阳的时候，停了一下，想了想，收起了神弓。嫦娥满意地看了后羿一眼，两人相对笑了。最后一个太阳慌张万分，也想像前面的太阳一样往海里跳。嫦娥喊道："请留下来，我们需要你！请按照天帝规定的时间起落，世间万物都会非常感谢你！"最后一个太阳脸红了，说："我以后再也不胡闹了！"

After completing the Emperor of Heaven's mission, Hou-Yi and Chang'E were to return to the Heavenly Palace.

On the way back, they saw that the Earth was in such bad shape that everywhere they went there were people moaning in despair and animals groaning in pain. Hou-Yi and Chang'E looked at each other and immediately knew that they were thinking the same – they could not just leave them behind like this. They both turned around to fly back to Earth.

Together they put out fires, looked for water sources, planted trees and built houses, to help the people rise from ashes.

完成了天帝的任务，后羿和嫦娥准备返回天宫了。上天的路上，他们低头一看，地面上创伤累累，远远还能听到一片呻吟之声。后羿和嫦娥互相看了一眼，都明白了对方心里想的是什么——他们不能就这样走了啊！于是，双双转身飞回地面。他们扑灭山火，寻找水源，又植树盖房，帮助人们从灰烬中站起来，重建家园。

Chang'E took many small homeless animals in and searched all over for herbs that could help cure their ailments.

A little white rabbit saved by Chang'E stayed around to help her prepare the medicines by pounding herbs in a mortar for her to make a paste to apply on the animals' wounds.

The rabbit was as white and pure as jade, so Chang'E named it "Jade Rabbit". She also called it "my little nurse" from time to time. Jade Rabbit stayed with Chang'E until after all the animals were cured.

嫦娥收留了很多无家可归的小动物，满山遍野寻找草药，亲自救治它们的伤痛。一只嫦娥用草药救活的小白兔，也留下来帮助嫦娥。它帮嫦娥把草药捣碎，敷在其它受伤的小动物身上。这只小白兔全身洁白如玉，嫦娥就给她起名叫"玉兔"，还常常叫她"我的小护士"。直到森林里的小动物们都恢复了健康，玉兔才恋恋不舍地离开嫦娥回家了。

A considerable amount of time had passed while the only sun left would dutifully rise and shine in the mornings and set and rest in the evenings. Trees grew back on hills, crops were planted again in fields, and rivers went back to running happily.

Stories about how Hou-Yi had shot the suns and saved the Earth were told from village to village. People's hearts were filled with gratitude for this hero.

By now, the nine suns shot down by Hou-Yi were all back at their father's palace with new jobs after their wounds were healed. One of the suns still hated Hou-Yi for what he had done to them, so he said many bad things about him to his father whenever he had a chance.

时间一天天过去，剩下的一个太阳早晨升起来，晚上落下去。山上长出树木，田里长出庄稼，江河重新奔流。人们怀着感激的心情，到处传颂着后羿射日的故事。被后羿射掉的九个太阳，回到天帝那里，都养好了伤，接受了新的任务。但其中一个太阳始终对后羿怀恨在心，一有机会就在天帝面前说后羿的坏话。

The Emperor of Heaven believed in what he was told and was very angry. Seeing that Hou-Yi took so long to come back, he got more upset with him and banished him from returning to Heaven.

The Emperor then sent an order to Chang'E to come back immediately. Chang'E's reply was: "If you don't take Hou-Yi back, please let me stay here with him." The Emperor was so mad that he ordered that Chang'E be demoted to a mortal as well.

Hou-Yi rushed to find Chang'E and urged her, "Please don't do this! Why would you trade being celestial with becoming mortal? A human can live for at most one hundred years!"

天帝听信了谗言，又看到后羿迟迟不归，就下令把后羿贬到人间，不许他再回到天庭，同时又下旨，让嫦娥速速回宫。嫦娥回复天帝说："如果不让后羿回去，请让我也留在这里吧。" 天帝大发雷霆，下令把嫦娥也贬下凡间。后羿得知，急得风风火火找到嫦娥，对她说："你这是何苦呢？放着神仙不做做凡人？做凡人那么辛苦，最长的寿命不过百年！"

Chang'E replied, "I can't leave! There is still so much for me to do on Earth. Plus, I don't think it is hard being a mortal. I am just happy to be with the person I love, even if only for one hundred years!"

Hou-Yi could not believe his ears. It was his dream coming true! He was so excited that he ran all the way to the top of the mountain and shouted on top of his lungs, "I — love — Chang'E!"

The valley echoed "Chang'E — Chang'E—" all the way around.

嫦娥说：“我不能离开啊，人间还有好多事情需要我做呢。而且我也不觉得做个凡人有多苦，能和自己喜欢的人在一起，我好幸福！哪怕只有一百年！”后羿几乎不敢相信自己的耳朵。简直是梦想成真！狂喜中，他飞奔跑上峰顶，向着丛山峻岭放声高喊：“我——爱——嫦娥——”山谷欢快的回声在天地间震荡：“嫦娥——嫦娥——”

Hou-Yi built a nice little house in the woods and the two got married, as humans.

On their wedding day, flowers blossomed, birds chirped, and animals cheered. People also gathered together, and danced and sang as if it was the most important holiday. Even some gods came down to Earth to congratulate the couple. Earth creatures and immortals from Heaven joined hand in hand in the biggest celebration of the forest.

后羿在森林中盖起了一座漂亮的小木屋，和嫦娥结为了夫妻。他们婚礼的那天，百花盛开，百鸟歌唱，百兽欢腾。人们也聚集过来，像欢庆节日一样载歌载舞。就连天神们也纷纷下凡，赶来为他们祝贺。草木、动物、凡人、神仙济济一堂，整个森林，成了一片欢乐的海洋。

Many young men on Earth admired Hou-Yi's arrow-shooting skills and came from near and far to learn this art from him. As more people came, Hou-Yi organized an arrow shooting team like he did in Heaven, and started regular training and competitions.

While Hou-Yi occupied himself teaching people how to make bows and arrows and later shoot them, Chang'E kept herself busy planting trees and flowers. She also built an animal hospital and sanctuary in their backyard to help care for small animals in need.

很多人间的小伙子佩服后羿百发百中的射箭绝技，从四面八方到这里来拜师学艺。后羿见学生越来越多，就组织起像在天庭一样的射箭运动队，进行训练和比赛。在后羿教人们制造弓箭、传授射箭本领的时候，嫦娥忙着在山上种树种花，还在小木屋的后面建起了动物医院和收容所，专门帮助和照顾小动物们。

Every evening after work, Hou-Yi would play his charming flute while Chang'E would dance her enchanting dance, drawing hundreds of people and animals nearby to come and watch.

Looking at his young and beautiful wife, Hou-Yi often felt guilty. It was for him that Chang'E had been turned from an immortal fairy to a regular human. Although they were leading a happy life together, youth and life as a human being was, after all, too short.

One day, Hou-Yi was thrilled to hear that the Queen Mother of Heaven had come down to Earth and made a magical potion on Mount Kun Lun, which could turn a human into an immortal capable of flying up to Heaven!

每天晚上，后羿坐在小木屋门前吹箫，嫦娥随着丈夫的箫声翩翩起舞，人们和小动物们都来观看。看着年轻美貌的妻子，后羿常常觉得非常内疚。正是为了他，嫦娥从天庭仙女变为一个凡间女子。虽然生活得幸福快乐，可是人类的青春和寿命毕竟太短暂了！有一天，后羿听说王母娘娘下凡到昆仑山巡访，她那里有一种神药，吃了可以上天，高兴得跳了起来。

Hou-Yi said goodbye to his wife and began his journey in search of the potion. He climbed ninety-nine high mountains and crossed ninety-nine wide rivers. After all the trials and hardships, he finally reached Mount Kun Lun and found the Queen Mother of Heaven.

Knowing that Hou-Yi and Chang'E were unjustly demoted to mortals, the Queen Mother took out a bottle of the magical potion and told Hou-Yi: "This is the only bottle I have left. If you take the whole thing, you'd be able to fly back up to Heaven. The Emperor has already forgiven you so it is OK to go back." "What if I split it with Chang'E?" Hou Yi asked. "Then neither of you could go back, but half of it will make you live and remain young forever, on Earth," the Queen Mother replied.

后羿告别了妻子，动身去求神药。翻过九十九座高山，游过九十九条大河，历尽千辛万苦，终于赶到了昆仑，找到了王母娘娘。王母深知后羿和嫦娥是受了委屈被贬到凡间的，便拿出神药，对后羿说，"我只有这一瓶药了，全都吃下它，你就能飞回天上去了。天帝早就原谅了你们！"后羿急切地问："那要是我和嫦娥分着吃呢？""那你们就谁都上不了天了。吃下一半，只能在人间长生不老。"

Hou-Yi rushed home with the magical potion. "Take it right away! Then you could go back to Heaven!" he told Chang'E. "But I'd only want to return with you! Why would I want to go back there by myself?" she replied.

"But there's only one bottle!" Hou-Yi sighed. "Why don't we split it in half and live together forever on Earth?" Chang'E smiled and said. "The human world will be as good as Heaven as long as I am with you!" Hou-Yi responded.

The two of them decided to take it together someday, before they grew old, so that both of them could live forever and keep each other company on Earth.

后羿拿到神药，飞奔回家，对嫦娥说："马上喝下这瓶药吧，你就能回到天庭了！"嫦娥说："要回我也要和你一起回，我一个人回去干什么！"后羿说："可是药只有一瓶啊！"嫦娥笑道："那可以一人吃一半，一起在地上生活啊！"后羿说："只要和你在一起，人间也像天堂一样！"于是，他们相约，在青春将逝的时候，两人一起吃下这个药，长生不老，永远相伴在人间。

Meanwhile, the people who had learned how to shoot arrows from Hou-Yi started to hunt and kill animals. When Hou-Yi played the flute and Chang'E danced, the small animals that used to watch them would flee at the sight of humans. The forest had lost its harmony and cheerfulness as before.

One day, a little white rabbit, chased by some people carrying bows and arrows, tripped and fell at Chang'E's doorstep. Oh no! It was Jade Rabbit, the "little nurse" who had helped her prepare medicine! Chang'E rushed over to pick it up in her arms, and couldn't hold back her tears.

人们学会了使用弓箭的本领之后，就开始到处狩猎，射杀小动物。后羿吹箫、嫦娥跳舞的时候，只要看到有人来，小动物们就四处逃散了，森林里失去了以往的和谐和欢乐。一天，一只小白兔被拿着弓箭的人们追赶着，摔倒在嫦娥家门口。天啊，这正是曾经帮她捣药的"小护士"玉兔啊！嫦娥赶紧抱起小白兔，眼泪扑簌簌地掉下来。

When Hou-Yi got home that evening, Chang'E said to him, "Please stop teaching people how to make and use bows and arrows. Look at how many poor creatures have been killed by them!"

"What does this have to do with me? I taught them how to make and use them, but I didn't teach them to kill animals with them!" Hou-Yi retorted.

The couple argued bitterly for a while. In the end, Hou-Yi wrapped up his covers and slept on the ground, while Chang'E sat in the bed, staring at the clean, bright moon outside the window for the whole night.

晚上，后羿一回家，嫦娥就对他说："不要再教人做弓箭，也不要教人射箭了！你看多少动物死在人的弓箭下啊，实在太可怜了！"后羿叫起来："这和我有什么关系！我教他们制作和使用弓箭，又没让他们用箭去杀死动物！"夫妻两个越吵越凶。后羿拿起被子睡到了地下。嫦娥坐在床上，望着窗外清静纯洁的月亮，一夜没合眼。

The next morning, when Hou-Yi was going to teach arrow shooting again, Chang'E stood by the door and begged him, "Please don't go. Please just destroy all the bows and arrows and bury them."

"Who are you kidding? You want me, the celestial arrow shooting champion, to destroy my own weapons with my own hands?" Hou-Yi raised his voice.

Tears in her eyes, Chang'E pleaded, "How could you bear to see more animals killed by humans with arrows? These animals have lives too, lives we have saved from the heat and fire!" Hou-Yi pushed Chang'E aside and left the house with his red bow and white arrow bag on his shoulders.

第二天早晨，后羿又要去教人们练习射箭。嫦娥在门口拦住了他，说："求你别再去了。把所有的弓箭都销毁了吧！""开什么玩笑！你让我后羿，天庭射箭冠军，去销毁弓箭？！"后羿高声说。嫦娥流下了眼泪："你就忍心看着人们用箭杀死动物吗？这些动物也是生命，和人类一样，是我们从火海中救出来的生命啊！"后羿一把推开嫦娥，背上他的大弓和箭袋，头也不回地走出了家门。

Chang'E held the white rabbit in her arms and cried her heart out. The whole day she was hearing small animals running for their lives, hunters' horses galloping, and arrows whizzing.

Chang'E sat by the window all day long. It happened to be Mid Autumn Day. When night fell, silvery moonlight poured through the window. Chang'E came out to the yard. The bright full moon was so pure and gentle that it soothed Chang'E's heart in pain.

嫦娥抱起小白兔，伤心得痛哭失声。整整一天，窗外不断地传来小动物拼命奔跑逃命的声音，猎人马蹄哒哒追捕的声音，根根利箭嗖嗖飞过的声音。嫦娥没吃也没喝，一直呆呆地站在窗口。这一天，正是中秋。夜幕降临了，银亮的月光照了进来。嫦娥来到院子里，一轮明月正在中天。月光是那样清纯、那样温柔，轻轻地抚摸着嫦娥痛苦的心。

Suddenly, all this peace and quiet was broken to pieces by laughing hunters with their captures loaded into full horse carriages. Drops of blood stained the moonlit ground as they tramped by.

Even the area in front of their little house where Chang'E had saved so many animals had now turned into a chilly killing ground. Even Hou-Yi, the world-saving hero, the love of her life, was becoming like a stranger.

What would Chang'E still care for in this world?

突然，一阵车欢马叫打破了月夜的宁静，狩猎的人们满载而归，哈哈大笑。他们走过之后，点点滴滴的鲜血留在了撒满月光的地面上。连自己救治了无数动物的小木屋前面，都不再是一片乐土，也不再是一片净土。后羿，拯救了众生的英雄，将要和自己天长地久、相伴终生的爱人，也变得如此陌生。这个世界，还有什么值得嫦娥留恋的呢？

Chang'E could not stand it any longer. She ran inside, opened the secret cabinet, and took out the potion from the Queen Mother of Heaven. "Good-bye, Hou-Yi!" Chang'E opened the bottle and gulped down the whole thing. A dizzy spell hit her and her body became as light as a feather as she started floating away from the ground.

Just then, she felt that she was stumbling on something. She lowered her head to take a look, and it was Jade Rabbit, holding on to the edge of her dress, its little red eyes looking up at her sadly. Chang'E knelt down to pick it up and flew off into the air.

嫦娥实在受不了了，她跑进内室，打开柜子，拿出了王母娘娘的神药。"再见了，后羿！"嫦娥打开药瓶，一口全吞了下去。一阵头晕目眩，嫦娥的身体突然感觉像羽毛一样轻飘飘的，整个人缓缓飘离了地面。突然，她感到脚下被什么东西绊住了，低头一看，玉兔正在抓住她的裙边，红红的小眼睛哀哀地看着她。嫦娥伏下身来，抱起小白兔，飘出了窗口。

Chang'E's heart ached as if it had been shot by a thousand arrows. Worrying about her husband and the small animals she cared for in the forests, Chang'E could not keep her eyes off her beloved home on Earth as it appeared farther and farther away from her.

All of a sudden, she saw a strong figure of a man marching on the road – it was Hou-Yi walking home after work. Something about him looked different. She squinted to look closely. She could not see his arrow bag, but only the big red bow in his hands – only the bow was broken in half! Chang'E could not help letting out a cry, "Oh no!"

嫦娥感到万箭穿心般的心痛。牵挂着丈夫，牵挂着家，牵挂着森林里的小动物们，嫦娥一步三回头。飘到小木屋的上方，嫦娥突然看到下面山坡上有一个魁梧的身影，那正是后羿！他正急匆匆大踏步走在回家的路上，看起来与往常有些不同。嫦娥眯起眼睛仔细望下去。后羿背后的箭袋不见了，手里拿着一把红色的大弓。噢，是一把被折断了的红色大弓！嫦娥失声叫了出来："后羿！"

Hearing this, Hou-Yi turned around to find his wife floating and flying up in the air. He couldn't help falling to the ground.

Chang'E had just realized that she had wronged her husband and wished she hadn't done what she had. Tears pouring, she struggled to turn back, calling, "Hou-Yi! Help me down!"

Hou-Yi jumped up to grab her waving sash in the air, but it quickly flew away from him as Chang'E floated farther away from the Earth. Whatever she tried, Chang'E was only able to fly upward, and she could never come back to Earth.

后羿听到叫声,猛然抬头一看,看到嫦娥正飞向天空,不由得两腿软软跪到了地上。嫦娥意识到自己错怪了丈夫,后悔得翻肠倒肚,泪如泉涌。她一边挣扎着向下飞,一边高喊:"后羿,快帮我!"后羿赶紧跳起来,伸手去抓嫦娥飘摆的裙带,可是,裙带越飘越高,嫦娥离地面越来越远,无论嫦娥怎么努力,她的身体只能向上飞,再也下不来了。

Hou-Yi was becoming smaller and smaller. Her eyes covered by tears, her heart breaking, her steps staggering, Chang'E did not know where she was or where she was going.

Where could she turn to in the endless sky? Back to the Heavenly Palace where there were her familiar gardens and palaces, her dear celestial sisters, and the heavenly music that she used to love to dance to? But no, Heaven was just too far from Earth!

地上的后羿已经越来越小了。嫦娥泪眼朦胧，肝肠寸断，在空中摇摇摆摆，跌跌撞撞，不知身在何处，不辨东西南北。茫茫天穹，浩瀚无边，她到哪里去呢？回到天宫？那里有她熟悉的琼楼玉宇，那里有她怀念的仙女姐妹，那里有她喜欢伴随起舞的天籁之音。可是，不能啊，天宫离地面太遥远了！

All the stars were winking at her as if trying to draw her attention to them. The North Star shone its bright spotlight on her. The Big Dipper played a cheerful tune on its guitar for her. But no. She could not. The stars were too far from where Hou-Yi was!

Suddenly, she saw the Moon, the round, bright, peaceful and cool Moon. Not having any of the luxuries of the Heavenly Palace, not having any of the charms of the welcoming stars, the Moon was, after all, the place in the sky that was closest to the Earth. Only from there could she still keep an eye on her home and her husband down below. Now that Chang'E had made up her mind, she started flying steadily towards the Moon.

满天的星宿都向她眨着眼睛。北极星亮起了欢迎的聚光灯，北斗七星弹起了快乐的长把吉他。可是，不能啊，星斗们离后羿太远了！突然，她看到了月亮！圆圆的、皎洁的月亮，安静的、冷清的月亮。没有天宫的极至繁华，没有群星的闪耀多情，但月亮毕竟是离地面最近的地方！只有在月亮上，天上人间可以遥遥相望。嫦娥下定了决心，直奔月亮飞去。

Meanwhile, Hou-Yi's heart was trembling with regrets. Like Chang'E, he also cherished every single life on Earth, or else he wouldn't have come thousands of miles across the vast space to save them; like Chang'E, he hated that the bows and arrows that he had introduced to this world had become hunting weapons that harmed Earth creatures. But why didn't he talk it over with his wife and tell her how he truly felt? Why did he have to argue with her like that?

Now she had left him, forever and ever! 'Chang'E, Chang'E, where are you?' he called in his heart.

后羿也后悔得捶胸顿足。他也和嫦娥一样，珍爱每一个生命，不然他不会飞越星空，到这里来解救灾难中的地球；他也和嫦娥一样，恨天上带来的弓箭在这里变成了杀害动物的凶器。可自己为什么不和嫦娥说清楚呢？为什么还要顶撞妻子呢？如今，性格刚烈的妻子离他而去了，而且是一去不复返了！嫦娥，嫦娥，你在哪儿？

Hou-Yi turned his eyes toward the night sky, and to his astonishment, he saw that the Moon was particularly bright tonight, and that there was a beautiful figure on it, dancing his wife's special dance! Hou-Yi was so familiar with Chang'E's one-of-a-kind moves that he could not possibly be mistaken. And what was the little thing by Chang'E's feet? Hou-Yi looked closely and made out that it was a rabbit. He ran home to find that Jade Rabbit was indeed gone.

Now separated like this, Hou-Yi could no longer tell Chang'E in person how much he had regretted what he had done and how much he was missing her.

后羿仰望夜空,突然惊奇地发现,今夜月亮特别明亮,月亮上有一个正在翩翩起舞的身影,那不正是嫦娥吗?!嫦娥的舞姿是那样独特,那样无可比拟的优美,后羿是再熟悉不过了!嫦娥旁边的小东西是什么?后羿定睛仔细一瞧,是一只小兔子!后羿赶紧跑回家里寻找,玉兔真的不见了。可是,天人相隔,后羿已经无法向妻子诉说自己的懊悔和思念了。

Up in the cold, lifeless Moon, facing the vast, endless sky, Chang'E was also suffering from remorse and could not sleep restfully at night. She could no longer hear her husband's gentle words. She could no longer help humans, care for animals or do things she liked. What would she do with this immortality in the sky if she could only live like this?

Now the only thing she could do was to swing her long, wide sleeves and dance Hou-Yi's favorite dance. Hopefully he could see her and tell from her sad movements that she, too, was missing him.

嫦娥在冷冷清清的月亮上，面对碧海青天，更被悔恨和孤独折磨得夜夜无法安眠。她再也不能听到丈夫温柔的话语了，她再也不能帮助人们和小动物们了，再也不能做自己喜欢的事情了。虽然人在天上，长生不老，又有什么意思呢？嫦娥只能甩起长长、宽宽的袖子，跳起后羿最喜欢的舞蹈。她想，也许这样后羿就会看到自己，也许这样后羿就能看出自己的悔恨和思念。

Hou-Yi did see and did understand how Chang'E felt. Ever since then, every year at the night of Mid Autumn Day when the Moon was its fullest, Hou-Yi would put Chang'E's favorite flowers and fruits out on the table in the garden.

Have you noticed that at every full moon, there is a beautiful figure in the Moon that changes its shape slowly? That, presumably, would be the dancing Chang'E. And the little figure by her side would be Jade Rabbit that keeps her company. If you look more closely, you'll probably also see that Jade Rabbit is still holding a mortar and crushing medicine!

后羿看到了，他明白了嫦娥的心。此后，每年的中秋，后羿就在院子里摆上嫦娥喜欢的鲜花水果，向嫦娥诉说思念之情。不知你注意看过没有，每个月圆之时，我们都能看到月亮上一个富于变化的优美身影，那就是翩翩起舞的嫦娥啊！还有一个小小的影子，那就是一直陪伴着嫦娥的玉兔啊！你要是再仔细看，还能看到玉兔拿着小罐子，还在不停地捣药呢！

Notes on Chinese Culture

1. The Queen Mother of Heaven
(王母娘娘, wáng mǔ niáng niang, P5, P23, P24, P33)

In Chinese mythology, the Queen Mother of Heaven is the Emperor of Heaven's mother. (Another variation is that she is his wife.) She is in charge of matters relating to obtaining immortality. She has a famous garden of magical peaches that would take three thousand years to come to blossom and fruit. Presumably, eating one of these peaches could make one live forever. She also experiments with and makes other sorts of potions and medicines of similar effects. She is in charge of entertaining the gods in Heaven as well as marital and childbirth matters of the gods and humans.

Being the mother of the Emperor of Heaven, she has almighty powers in Heaven and on Earth.

2. Mid Autumn Day
(中秋节, zhōng qiū jié, P30, P44)

Mid Autumn Day, also called the "Moon Festival", is celebrated on the fifteenth day of the eighth month by lunar calendar, which often falls on the later half of September of the Western calendar. Moon worshipping traced back to a few thousand years ago in China.

Mid Autumn Day has also been considered a harvest festival, since fruits, vegetables and grain have been harvested by this time and food is abundant. Traditionally, people would place food offerings on an altar set up in the courtyard and sit around drinking and eating in the moonlight. (This might have originated from Hou-Yi's offerings to Chang'E.) Typical food offerings were all kinds of fruits and moon cakes (月饼).

Moon cakes, measuring about three inches in diameter and one and a half inches in thickness, resemble Western fruitcakes in taste and consistency. They are often stuffed with melon seeds, lotus seeds, almonds, minced meats, bean paste, orange peels, and lard. Often a golden yolk from a salted duck egg is placed at the center of each cake, and the golden brown crust is usually decorated with symbols of the festival.

Nowadays, giving friends and family moon cakes with exquisite packaging before the Moon Festival has become more and more popular among the Chinese population. The Moon Festival has become more of a special day of family reunion, when families and friends get together for a big feast. In many ways it is very similar to Thanksgiving in some Western countries.

3. Evolution of Some Chinese Characters

Many Chinese characters have evolved from images, namely, drawings of the object or action described by the character. See below how some characters from this story have evolved to the way they are now.

the Sun	☉	日	日	(rì)
the Moon	☽	月	月	(yuě)
mountain	⛰	山	山	(shān)
water	〣	水	水	(shuǐ)
wood	木	木	木	(mù)
human	人	人	人	(rén)

Notes on the Series

The *Enchanted Tales of China* series, as part of the *Golden Peach Chinese Culture Readers* program, collects and retells the most treasured, timeless Chinese tales that have captured hearts and imaginations for over a thousand years.

● **Bilingual Text**
Each old story is retold in modern English for general Western readers interested in Asian cultures. In addition, the English text is supplemented by text in Chinese on the bottom of page for readers who wish to learn more of the language, or as a helpful tool for Chinese teachers or parents.

● **Leveled Format**
The series is loosely leveled for different age groups, based on their various abilities in understanding the culture, rather than their language levels. To give readers ample room for flexibilities, the levels are not distinctly marked with numbers, but only color coded for easy recognitions: the orange level targets mostly teenage readers, and the green level is more for younger children.

● **Cultural Notes**
Notes on Chinese culture will enhance readers' understanding of the stories, as well as of their historical and social backgrounds. For older readers the notes are more elaborate and detailed, while for younger audience they come in a simple format under a section entitled "Did you know...?"

● **Color Illustrations**
Full color, vibrant illustrations highlight some important scenes.